FOR DAD

First published 2017 by Walker Books Ltd
87 Vauxhall Walk, London SE11 5HJ

© 2017 Sam Zuppardi

The right of Sam Zuppardi to be identified as the
author and illustrator of this work has been asserted by him
in accordance with the Copyright, Designs and Patents Act 1988

This book has been typeset in Egyptian Extended,
Just Another Hand, and Kids Crayon.

Printed in China

British Library Cataloguing in Publication Data:
a catalogue record for this book is available from the British Library

ISBN 978-1-4063-7694-4

www.walker.co.uk

THINGS TO DO WITH Dad

Sam Zuppardi

WALKER BOOKS

AND SUBSIDIARIES

LONDON · BOSTON · SYDNEY · AUCKLAND

THINGS TO DO

WASH THE DISHES

BUILD THE BOOKCASE

HOOVER THE CARPETS

MAKE THE BEDS

HANG OUT THE LAUNDRY

WATER THE GARDEN

HOOVER THE CARPETS

THINGS TO DO
With Dad

~~WASH THE DISHES~~

~~BUILD THE BOOKCASE~~

~~OOVER THE CARPETS~~

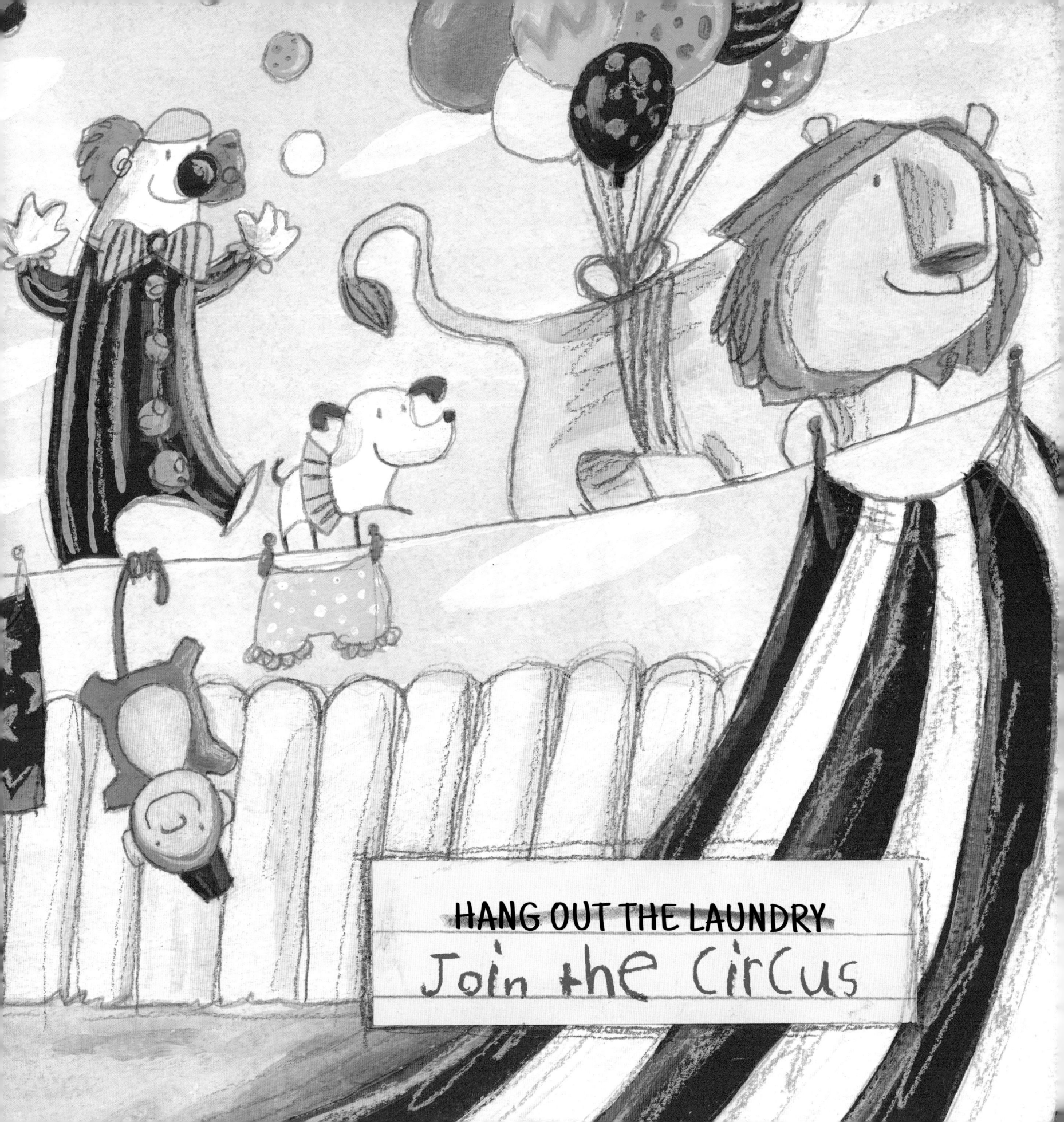

HANG OUT THE LAUNDRY
Join the Circus